SPANISH PIONEERS
OF THE SOUTHWEST

SPANISH PIONEERS OF THE SOUTHWEST

by Joan Anderson

photographs by George Ancona

LODESTAR BOOKS   E. P. DUTTON   NEW YORK

Other books by Joan Anderson
with photographs by George Ancona

Christmas on the Prairie

The First Thanksgiving Feast

The Glorious Fourth at Prairietown

Joshua's Westward Journal

Pioneer Children of Appalachia

A Williamsburg Household

Library of Congress Cataloging-in-Publication Data

Anderson, Joan.
  Spanish pioneers of the Southwest.
  "Lodestar books."
  Summary: Re-creates in text and photographs the day-to-day life
of a pioneer family living in a newly formed Spanish settlement
in the Southwest during the eighteenth century.
  1. Southwest, New—History—to 1848—Juvenile literature.
2. Spaniards—Southwest, New—History—18th century—Juvenile
literature. 3. Frontier and pioneer life—Southwest, New—
Juvenile literature. [1. Southwest, New—History. 2. Frontier
and pioneer life—Southwest, New] I. Ancona, George, ill.
II. Title.
F799.A53 1988 979 88-16121
ISBN 0-525-67264-8

Published in the United States by
E. P. Dutton, New York, N.Y.,
a division of NAL Penguin Inc.

Published simultaneously in Canada by
Fitzhenry & Whiteside Limited, Toronto

Editor: Rosemary Brosnan   Designer: Robin Malkin

Printed in the U.S.A.   First Edition
10 9 8 7 6 5 4 3 2 1

to Marc Simmons, *muchas gracias*

J.A.

Dedico este libro a mi familia—
los Ancona-Diaz.   G.A.

Twenty years before the Pilgrims arrived on the east coast of North America, Don Juan de Onates led troops and settlers into the northern portion of New Spain (which is now New Mexico) to establish not only the first Spanish colony in North America but, more importantly, the first colony of Europeans in the New World. They crossed the Atlantic, landed on the east coast of Mexico (part of New Spain), and eventually traveled northward, where they were granted large parcels of land in exchange for setting up a Spanish community. In 1610, Don Pedro de Peralta founded Santa Fe and made it the capital of the new lands belonging to Spain. By the 1650s, many Spanish settlements were being established in the Southwest. The king of Spain dictated how the settlements should look and insisted that settlers build *torreones,* or round, high forts, in all of them.

This book is about one such place—El Rancho de las Golondrinas. It was owned in the 1650s by Manuel Vega y Coca and eventually fell into the hands of the Baca family. We will experience life as it was in the mid 1700s when Golondrinas was inhabited by fifty or so Baca family members. Aside from being a self-sufficient fort where the Bacas farmed and raised sheep, Golondrinas was also a hotel, or hacienda, for traders, military expeditions, and other travelers along the dangerous Camino Real.

These first colonists clung firmly to their Hispanic culture and language. Their spirit has left an indelible mark on the attitudes, values, religion, and customs of the Southwest.

The only reward in collecting wood today, Miguel thought, was that soon there would be a fiesta celebrating the coming of spring. Mamá and the other women of Golondrinas needed all the firewood that could be gathered to light the *hornos* and kitchen fireplaces. Miguel's stomach growled at the thought of food—the *dulces*, the green corn, and especially his favorite dish, *panocha*. He had left the hacienda at dawn with only a loaf of bread and some water. The sun was already making its westward descent toward the Sandría Mountains, which was Miguel's sign to head home.

"Come on, Gaspar," he said, nudging his faithful burro. "We've been out here long enough." Miguel tugged at his burro's reins and led Gaspar down the hillside into the valley. They trudged across the great dusty plains that served as the hacienda's backyard.

Miguel walked carefully and deliberately. He didn't want to tangle with any rattlesnakes coiled inconspicuously around desert brush, or Navajo scouts who spied on the Spanish settlers from nearby mesas.

Just last year, Miguel's brother Pedro had been taken captive in a Navajo raid. Miguel lived in fear of meeting the same fate. He shuddered every time he recalled that awful day.

All the villagers had scrambled to safety at the sound of the bell. Pedro too had run, but his pace was slowed because he carried with him a baby lamb. Miguel had watched helplessly as a Navajo scooped up his brother and rode away.

"Hurry up, Gaspar," he ordered, now more anxious than ever to get home.

It was difficult to see the hacienda from a distance, because the brown adobe fortress blended right into the landscape. Squinting hard, he finally spotted it and quickened his step, pushing Gaspar's hind end up the very last hill.

"Finally!" Miguel sighed as they approached the pine gate. "I return, Mamá," he bellowed triumphantly.

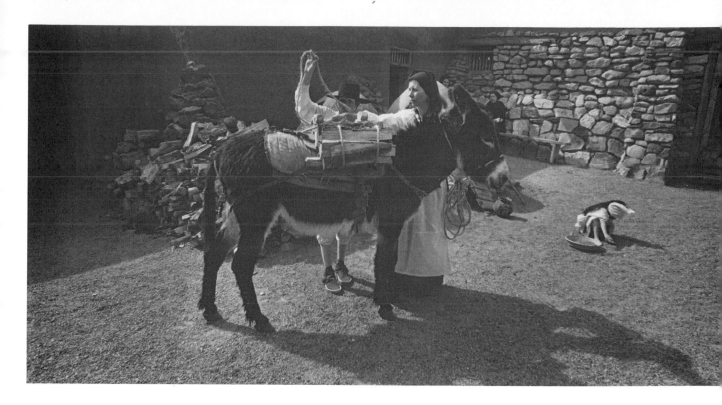

"Such a big load, Miguel!" his mother exclaimed. "And you've even cut the wood this time. *Bueno. Bueno.* Here, let me help you."

Miguel smiled at his mother's welcome. There was such relief in her eyes at his safe return. Miguel was the only Baca child old enough to help around the hacienda. His little sister, Rosa, spent her days at play, and baby Juan was just six weeks old.

Everywhere in the *placita* the people of Golondrinas were busy working. Because Nueva Mexico was so far away from any city, they had to make everything they needed for daily life.

Doña María, the *patrón*'s wife, was brightening up a simple muslin *colcha* with embroidery, while her husband, Don Hernando, was working over the wooden loom, weaving fabric from which heavy blankets and ponchos would be fashioned. Margarita, the *patrón*'s sister, was carding freshly sheared lamb's wool, and Tía Lupita, Miguel's aunt, was hanging goat's-milk cheese from the beams in the cool storage room, where fruits and vegetables were being dried.

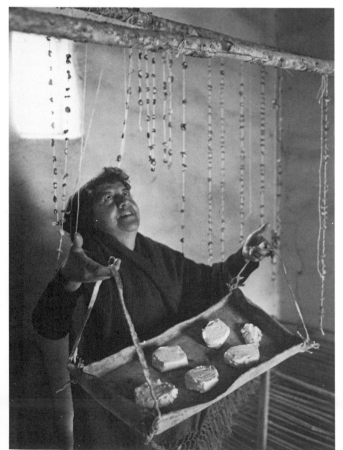

Just as Miguel was about to settle into a warm corner and rest his weary limbs, his father approached.

"Miguel, you've returned," he exclaimed. "I've been scanning the land all afternoon in hopes of spotting you," he said, gesturing at the wilderness beyond the gate. "You must not have met up with any grizzlies this time?" Emilio Baca joked.

"No, Papá, I didn't go up on the mesa. But if I had, I would have been ready with my knife."

"If you weren't near the mesa, wherever did you find so many juniper and piñon branches?"

"The hills west of here, Papá."

"West!" his father said. "That's getting close to Navajo country!"

"I know, Papá, but I stay alert and so far I haven't seen one Indian."

"You're becoming very brave, Miguel," his father continued, shaking his head in amazement at his young son. "The *patrón* says that he wants to give you duty in the *torreón*."

"Me?" Miguel gasped. "Stand watch like a soldier? Do you think I'm able?" he asked, straightening his spine and feeling a new rush of energy.

"Anyone who braves mesa tops and can fend off grizzly bears is man enough to guard our home. Come, enough talk," Emilio Baca said, putting his arm around his son's shoulder. "It's time for our meal. I will remind the *patrón* of his suggestion, but not until you have helped in plowing the field. The past few years your brother Pedro helped me. Now that he is gone I must look to you, Miguel."

It was warm and cozy in the Bacas' *cocina*. The chili stew smelled delectable as the family gathered and Abuelita Luisa dished it up. Everyone sat quietly, exhausted but content to be slowing down from the toils of the day.

The chill of the night descended upon them. Emilio Baca built up the fire as his wife, Isabel, unrolled the blankets and sheepskins that would become their beds. Miguel's father took his place atop the fireplace, and the others huddled close to the hearth.

Miguel felt his muscles relax as his mother began to sing softly to the baby. For the first time all day, Miguel knew he was safe. Only here in the cozy *cocina* did he feel he could let his guard down. He couldn't let Papá know that he wasn't all that brave. So on the outside, Miguel stood tall and proud, but on the inside he trembled with fear.

Dawn came early. With only a few tiny windows in the Bacas' *cocina,* it was impossible to know when the sun came up. But the *patrón* took care that the people of Golondrinas were alerted to the early hour by ringing the hacienda's huge iron bell.

Miguel stirred upon hearing the dull clang. One. Two. Three. Four. Five. On the fifth ring he bolted upright. Glancing about the room he saw that Papá's bed was vacant! Was he already at work? Miguel quickly rolled up his blanket, gulped down a cup of *atole,* and headed out the door.

Sure enough, Papá was down by the stream near the small plot of cultivated farmland. Miguel ran as fast as he could, anxious to show his father that even though he wasn't as big and strong as Pedro, he was eager to work.

"I'm here, Papá," he announced. "What shall I do?"

"Quickly, grab hold of the yoke while I secure it to their horns. These beasts want nothing of work this morning."

Miguel did as his father said, and eventually they attached the crude wooden plow and headed for the far end of the field. The earth was hard and dry. Miguel was always amazed that things grew in such unhealthy-looking soil.

"Papá," he asked, his teeth chattering in the early morning chill, "isn't it still too cold for planting?"

"It would seem so, my son," Emilio Baca answered as the plowshare dug into the soil and began to turn the earth. "But we must hope that the days soon become warm, as it takes many months to grow our corn and beans and wheat. Besides, Padre José will come to bless our fields during the Feast of San Ysidro. If we haven't done our work there can be no blessing, *sí*?"

"I suppose not, Papá," Miguel answered, working steadily now. It felt good to be sharing chores with someone instead of being alone tending sheep and collecting wood. Time passed quickly, and by late afternoon they were putting in the seed. Miguel felt proud of their accomplishment, especially since the *patrón* had been watching their progress from the rooftop of the hacienda.

Just as Miguel was placing the last of the seeds in the carefully dug holes, a voice called to him. "Miguel, come give me a hand."

Miguel dropped the seed bag and ran. Whenever the *patrón* had a request, the villagers obliged. He was, after all, the owner of Golondrinas—the person to whom they all turned for food and favors. It was an honor to help him in return.

"Look how full our stream is, after the winter's snow," he said, his voice booming, as it always did, with great joy. "We must open up the irrigation ditch, *sí*, Miguel? Your newly planted seeds will be crying for moist soil."

"*Sí, señor,*" Miguel answered, grabbing a long stick and pushing with all his might the board that held the water back. Suddenly it gave way and the sparkling-clean water gushed forth, heading straight for the field.

"We must make good use of this water, my boy, since we have so very little, *sí*?" The *patrón* slapped Miguel on the back, pleased that another job was done.

"Come, let's head back to the hacienda," the *patrón* said to his young helper.

During the next few days, Miguel went about his regular chores hoping that soon the *patrón* would remember his promise and permit him to stand watch in the *torreón*.

Each morning he tossed fresh straw into the corral for the barn animals to eat. He fed the chickens and turkeys, milked the goats, and held the sheep steady while they were sheared.

In the afternoons, sometimes with his father, sometimes alone, he took the sheep to the nearby hills to graze. The days were long and hard, and Miguel began to wonder why there seemed to be more work this spring than in other years. Then he realized—Pedro wasn't there this year to share in all the work.

One afternoon, while he mixed the reddish-brown earth with straw and water to make adobe bricks, Miguel heard the thunder of hooves as a horse galloped toward the hacienda. Jumping to attention, he shielded his eyes from the dust and watched as a Pueblo Indian passed by.

The Pueblos were a friendly people whom the Spanish settlers had learned to cooperate with. They brought pottery, baskets, and fruit to the hacienda to exchange for sheepskins and sugar. Miguel marveled at how the Pueblo men wore little clothing and seemed unaffected by the cold weather. He crept up to the pine gate and nestled unobtrusively in the corner, hoping to eavesdrop on Margarita's conversation. Miguel took any chance he could to understand the mysterious world of the Indians, especially now that his brother was part of that world.

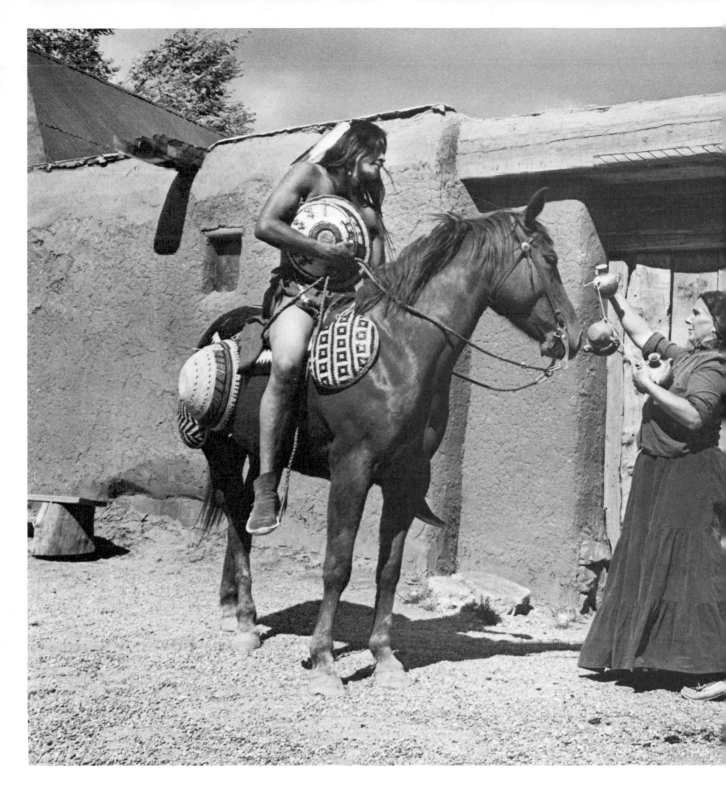

"Have you visited any Navajo villages of late?" Margarita whispered to the Pueblo. Miguel moved closer as the Pueblo nodded yes. "By chance did you spot our beloved Pedro?" she pressed.

"No, no, no," he answered, a sad tone to his voice.

"Well then," she said, trying to cover up her disappointment, "let us see what you have brought today."

Miguel watched as the Indian showed Margarita brightly colored baskets and sturdy pottery jugs, but his interest in Indian things had been suddenly dampened.

"If only I were big enough to go off and find Pedro," Miguel said, sighing. "Perhaps when I learn to handle the muskets in the *torreón* I will be able to rescue him."

The very next morning the *patrón*, Don Hernando, stopped by the Baca *cocina* and assigned Miguel to the morning watch.

His head brimming with thoughts of fighting off Indians, and his heart pounding at the thought of a dramatic rescue of his brother, Miguel climbed the rickety ladder leading to the tower. Feeling like his conquistador ancestors, he stepped out into the open and gazed over the rugged landscape. He felt nervous about the responsibility given to him. Pacing about behind the small parapet, he rehearsed in his mind just what he was supposed to do in case of attack.

The strains of the *alabados* being
sung by the women in the chapel
beneath him caused Miguel to relax a
bit, knowing that prayers were being
offered for protection from the forces
of evil.

In the distance he could see the Indian servant, Polonia, with her little girl trailing behind, fetching water from the stream. For the first time Miguel wondered what had possessed the *patrón* to take Polonia captive, and why she now seemed so content with the Spanish way of life. Didn't she miss the Indian ways? Could Pedro be experiencing the same thing? Might he be taking to the Navajo way of life? There was so much Miguel didn't understand.

It was almost noon and soon Miguel would be relieved of his duty. As he did one last turn on the *torreón,* he saw something far off in the distance. Squinting and shielding his eyes from the glistening sun, he focused on the spot to make sure his imagination wasn't playing tricks on him. The speck became larger, and the hairs on the back of his neck began to stand on end. Momentarily, Miguel froze. But as the speck billowed into a cloud of dust, he could only conclude that a band of marauders was approaching. Without another thought, he shouted, "Indians! I see Indians!" There was a terror in his voice that he didn't know he felt. "Sound the bell!" he shouted to a village boy who was nearby.

Miguel watched the villagers pause as they counted the number of rings. Everyone knew that three clangs meant danger. They dropped their tools and came running from every direction.

"Hurry, Papá," Miguel called to his father, who was in the newly planted field. He glanced down into the *placita* to look for the rest of his family. Mamá was cuddling Juan to her breast, and Rosa was playing nearby, oblivious to the commotion.

But where was Abuelita Luisa? Suddenly Miguel remembered seeing her bent over in the herb garden. He clambered down the ladder and raced out of the *placita* to help her. She couldn't run as fast as the others, and he couldn't bear the thought of having another member of his family captured. He had gone only a few steps when she came around the corner. Miguel extended his hand and pulled her inside.

"Now," the *patrón* shouted, "close the gate." The men bolted it with a huge pine beam while the women huddled inside the *torreón*. And then everyone waited.

A deadly silence fell over Golondrinas as they listened for the intruders. Miguel could hear his heart beating. He clutched at his pocket to make sure his knife was still there and noticed an ax lying near the woodpile. He felt better knowing there were weapons within reach.

Would the Indians scale the walls and jump from the roof into the *placita*? Miguel wondered. Why didn't they hear war cries? What was happening? He dared not ask and instead searched his father's face for some clues. Just then there was a *jingle jangle* of metal. Next he heard the creaking of heavy cottonwood wheels and the *clop, clop, clop* of some domestic animal. The women were peering out the tiny window in the wall of the *torreón* when one of them exclaimed: "It is only Don Carlos!"

The *patrón* opened the small door first to make sure the women weren't seeing things. Sure enough, there stood Carlos, his *carreta* loaded with supplies he had brought from Mexico City to sell.

"Open up the gates," the *patrón* shouted, "and let our good friend in!"

"*Bienvenido, mi amigo,*" the *patrón* said, hugging the merchant tightly. "We are happier to see you than you can imagine." He grinned, winking at Miguel.

The merchant was not used to such a greeting and seemed puzzled. He stayed beside his *carreta* until the *patrón* urged him inside. "Come in, señor. *Mi casa es su casa!*"

In all the excitement, the villagers had failed to see the other surprise that awaited them. Padre José had also arrived, having met up with Carlos on El Camino Real, the King's Highway.

"Padre, you are here as well," the *patrón* shouted in greeting. The *patrón* turned to Emilio Baca. "Finally your baby will be baptized, Emilio. You won't have to worry anymore about such things, *sí*?"

Miguel's father grinned and shook the padre's hand. Golondrinas had not seen such excitement in a long time.

Suddenly the quiet hacienda turned into a noisy little town as the women gathered around Carlos, anxious to see the goods he had brought from Mexico City.

"Did you bring any mantillas?" Doña María asked eagerly. "I long for a new piece of lace upon my head, especially since I wear a mantilla every day for prayers."

"There may be just one left," Carlos answered, a teasing twinkle in his eye as he slowly rummaged through one of his many barrels. "Will this do?" he asked, dramatically waving a single piece of lace in front of the señora's face.

"Muy bien!" she exclaimed, delight lighting up her tired-looking face.

Meanwhile, Margarita carefully eyed all that Carlos had un-packed and arranged on the blanket. In one hand he held lumps of sweet brown sugar, a delicacy the hacienda had been without for months. There were bolts of fabric, a beautiful satin gown, badly needed iron tools, and a candle holder. Just looking at the array of such things reminded the settlers of what they had left behind when they moved here from Mexico.

That night, Doña María and Isabel Baca made a grand meal, as they always did when visitors stopped off at the hacienda. For the first time, Miguel was invited to join the men at the table.

"What a journey!" Carlos said as he settled in at his place and gulped down some red wine. "What a journey."

Miguel leaned forward as the merchant began to talk. Carlos always had a colorful adventure to report. Even if his journey had been uneventful, Carlos would make it sound treacherous. "Padre," he began, "it is a miracle that I sit here. I came upon quicksand near the Rio Grande and it all but swallowed me up." He took another swig of wine. "Someday soon," Carlos continued, "I'll settle down on your hacienda, Don Hernando, and give up this merchant life. I'm too old for such adventures. Perhaps, Miguel, you would want to take over my job, *sí*?" Don Carlos teased, "and I'll tend your sheep."

Miguel gasped at the very thought of such an adventurous life. "Papá," he exclaimed, turning toward his father who had just entered the room, "you're just in time. Carlos wants me to learn his business!"

"And leave all your new responsibilities behind?" his father asked. "Miguel is now standing watch like all the other men at Golondrinas," his father said proudly, staring straight at the merchant.

"Is that so, Miguel," the old man said quickly, sensing that he had stirred up the pot enough for one night. "Well then, you'd best stay put here for another few years, *sí*?"

"Well, now that that's decided," Doña María concluded, clearing her throat in an effort to divert attention, "take this pot of stew down to the soldiers, Miguel. Once again they managed to keep our supply route safe, and I'm sure they would like some home-cooked food."

Miguel had all but forgotten about the soldiers. Sure enough, as he headed down the hillside, he saw their tents neatly set up just outside the pine gate. He ran down the hill, eager to hear tales of war and adventure.

The next morning, all regular chores were put aside so that the villagers could prepare for the festival. Padre José was needed in other settlements and would stay for only a day or two.

The saint maker of Golondrinas had been working day and night in anticipation of the padre's arrival. His beautiful carving of San Ysidro plowing the fields was almost complete. Miguel loved to watch as he mixed brightly colored paints from different plants and chipped away at a block of wood until the block disappeared and in its place was a magnificent figure. Tomorrow San Ysidro, the patron saint of farmers, would be carried about the hacienda on his way to the little chapel. From this spot, high above Golondrinas, he would bless and watch over the fields until harvest.

Nearby, Doña María was hunched over a bunch of dried chilis, picking out the seeds and grinding them into powder. Blue corn would be ground as well to make flour for all the tortillas that would be consumed at the fiesta. Polonia stood patiently beside the *hornos* waiting for the *dulces* to bake. Everyone loved the sweet-tasting bread that was made for special occasions.

Finally, it was May 15; the Feast of San Ysidro was upon them.

A procession formed and the crowd moved slowly out of the great pine gate. Carrying the statue of San Ysidro on their shoulders, they wove their way down the hillside to the precious irrigation ditch, around the newly planted field of crops, through the pasture, until finally they approached the chapel. They chanted as they walked.

> San Ysidro, land tiller
> Protect our crops
> From pests and storms
> San Ysidro, golden whiskered
> Pray to God
> To send us rain in torrents

Miguel watched as they placed the wooden saint gently on the altar of the tiny church. From there, San Ysidro could watch the hacienda and all of its people.

After the ceremony, the padre stood off to the side, his mind deep in thought.

"Padre," Miguel said, "already since your arrival it seems to me that the soil looks richer."

"My boy," Padre José answered, "this is good land that God has given to us to settle upon. If we care for it, taking only what we need, as our Pueblo Indian neighbors do, it will serve us with abundance."

"Hurry to the corral," Miguel called out to all those in the hacienda. "Padre is preparing to bless our animals."

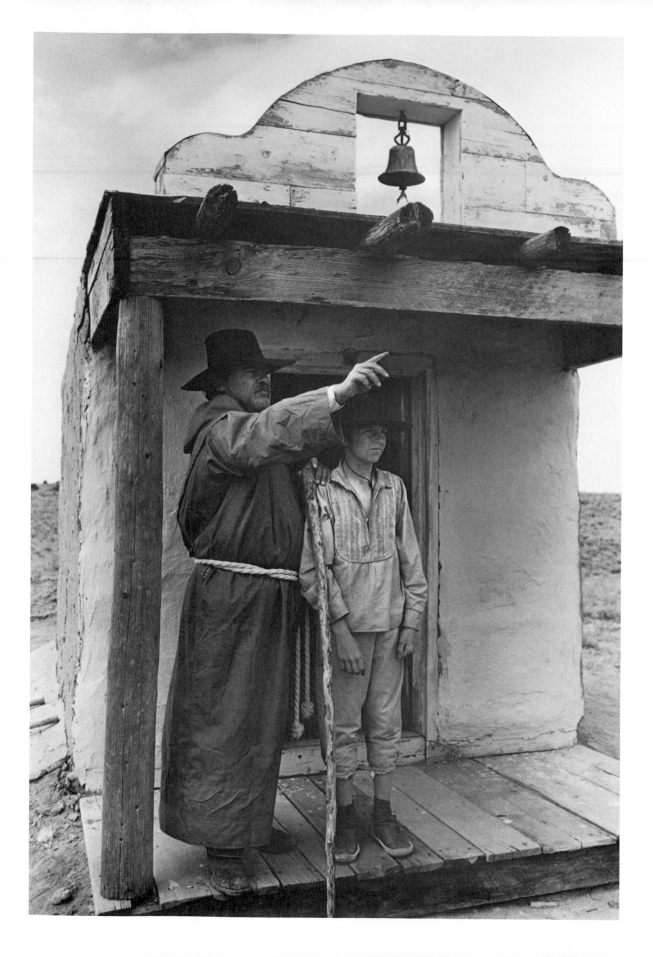

GLOSSARY

abuelita (ah-bway-LEE-tah) grandma

alabado (ah-lah-BAH-doe) praise of the Host sung in the Catholic Church

atole (ah-TOE-lay) corn-flour gruel

Bienvenido, mi amigo (Bee-en-vay-NEE-doe, mee ah-MEE-goe) Welcome, my friend

bueno (BWAY-noe) good

carreta (cah-RREH-tah)* ox cart

cocina (coe-SEE-nah) kitchen

colcha (COHL-chah) quilt, bedspread

conquistador (con-KEE-stah-door) conqueror; one of the Spanish conquerors of Mexico and Peru in the sixteenth century

corrida (coh-RREE-dah)* a popular song from the region of Andalusia in Spain

don (don) Spanish title used before a man's first name as a mark of respect

doña (DOH-nyah) Spanish title used before a woman's first name as a mark of respect

dulce (DOOL-say) sweet (dessert)

El Camino Real (El Cah-MEE-noe Ray-AHL) The King's Highway

fiesta (fee-ES-tah) feast; holiday; feast day

golondrina (goe-lon-DREE-nah) swallow (bird)

hacienda (ah-see-EN-dah) ranch

horno (OR-noe) oven

jota (HOH-tah) Spanish dance

mantilla (mahn-TEE-yah) a silk or lace head scarf worn by Spanish women and Latin American women of Spanish descent

mesa (MAY-sah) plateau

Mi casa es su casa (Mee CAH-sah es soo CAH-sah) My house is your house (a polite expression used very commonly among Spanish speakers)

muy bien (mwee bee-EN) very well

padre (PAH-dray) father; priest

panocha (pah-NOE-cha) corn pudding; ear of Indian corn

patrón (pah-TRONE) landlord; male boss

patrona (pah-TROH-nah) landlady; female boss

placita (plah-SEE-tah) little plaza

poncho (PON-choe) a blanketlike cloak with a hole in the center for the head

señor (seh-NYOR) sir; Mr.

señora (seh-NYO-rah) madam; Mrs.

sí (see) yes

tía (TEE-ah) aunt

torreón (toe-rray-OWN)* large fortified tower

tortilla (tor-TEE-yah) a thin, round, unleavened bread usually made from corn meal

---

*The double *r* is a sound made by rolling the tongue; *rr* is a letter in Spanish.

Note: The words listed in this glossary have been defined as they are used in this book. Some of them also have other meanings. For additional definitions, look the words up in a Spanish-English dictionary.

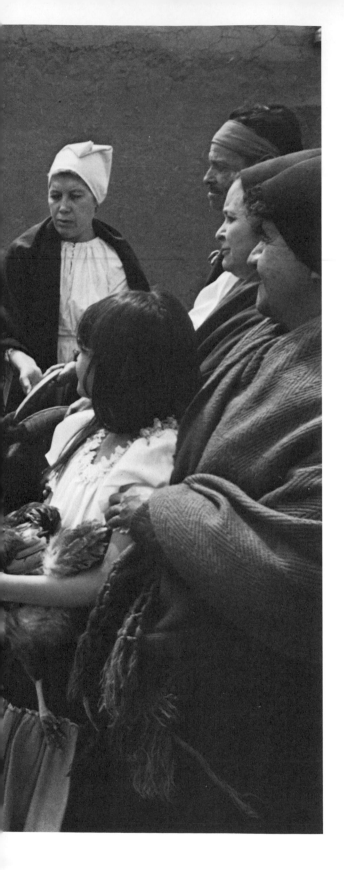

Miguel watched as goats and roosters, lambs and geese were gathered up and taken to this very special service.

"But where is Gaspar?" he said. Of all the animals that meant something to Miguel, Gaspar was the most important. Miguel felt more protected when he roamed the countryside with Gaspar as his companion. Miguel knew that if they encountered trouble it would be Gaspar who got them out of it.

"Never mind about Gaspar!" Miguel's father said. "Hold on to the baby goat. He was born only last week."

Suddenly there was a hush. Even the animals calmed down, perhaps sensing the solemnity of the moment. Miguel realized once again how much every one of the animals was needed . . . for food, for transportation and work—even for clothing.

"Blessings on the animals," he said, repeating the words of Padre José as the priest sprinkled the animals with holy water.

With the major ceremonies behind them, the settlers of Golondrinas began their much-deserved fiesta. They celebrated their hard work and survival by singing the *corridas* of Spain and dancing the *jota,* and of course feasting on all the delicacies the women had prepared.

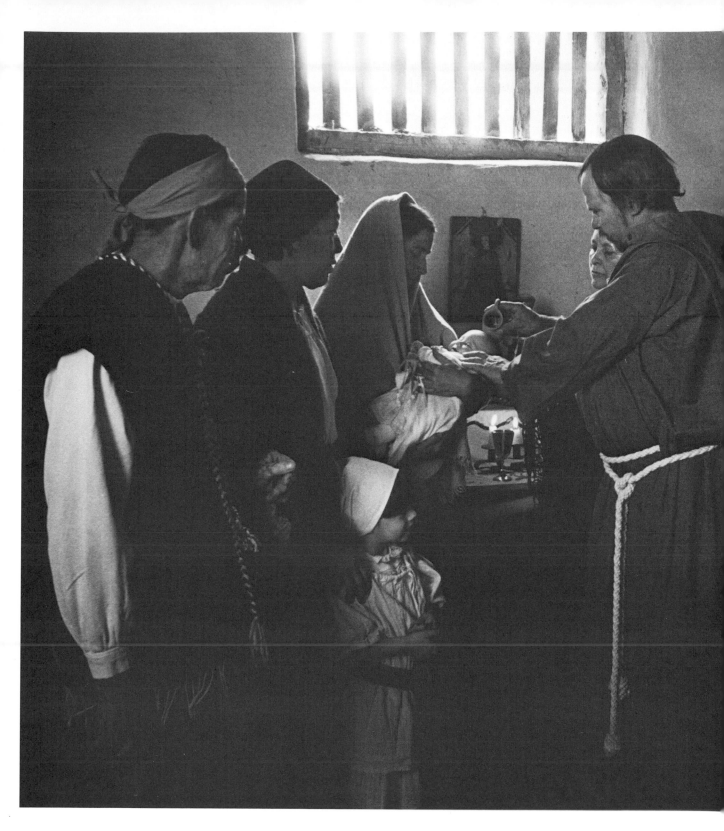

During the afternoon, Padre José ushered the Baca family into their tiny family chapel to baptize little Juan. Miguel watched from a corner as Mamá and Papá gathered round the altar with Abuelita Luisa nearby and the *patrón* and *patrona,* who were to be godparents. The baby squirmed as the blessings were said, and everyone beamed at this precious creature. Only Pedro was missing, Miguel thought. But the baby brought joy to his mamá's eyes. For that Miguel was grateful. Today everything seemed new and hopeful, just like the season of spring itself.

ACKNOWLEDGMENTS

The photographs for this book were taken on location at El Rancho de las Golondrinas. The people playing the roles of the Baca family are actors who reenact what life was like for the Spanish pioneers.

Rita and George Palheimo opened the doors of Golondrinas to our cameras and thus made it possible to expose this little-known part of American history. The book enjoys historical accuracy because of hours of conversation, interviews, and reading materials given to the author by Dr. Marc Simmons. Cassie Vieira was invaluable in helping with everything from casting the characters to providing props. And then we owe our deepest gratitude to the hardworking actors who stayed with us for an entire week and let us tell this story. Particularly special to this project were Rogelio Ramirez and Maria Ramirez, who put in many long hours. We are grateful to Michael Garcia, who wasn't sure what he was getting into at the onset of the week and became a stellar actor by the end. Thanks to all the other actors: Lytning Elk; William Simbola, Margo Simbola and their little daughter; Jake Montoya; Alan Tobin; Domingo Perea; John Palheimo; Kimberly Gonzales; and baby Amelia Vanderlaan.

ABOUT THE AUTHOR AND PHOTOGRAPHER

JOAN ANDERSON and GEORGE ANCONA have collaborated on many award-winning books. Among them are *The First Thanksgiving Feast* and *A Williamsburg Household*. About this book, Joan Anderson says, "The Spanish influence on the United States should be drawn upon and rejoiced about." George Ancona, who is Mexican-American, says, "It enabled me to hear a bit of the story, sounds, and music of my history."

Author Joan Anderson lives in Pearl River, New York. Photographer George Ancona lives in Stony Point, New York.